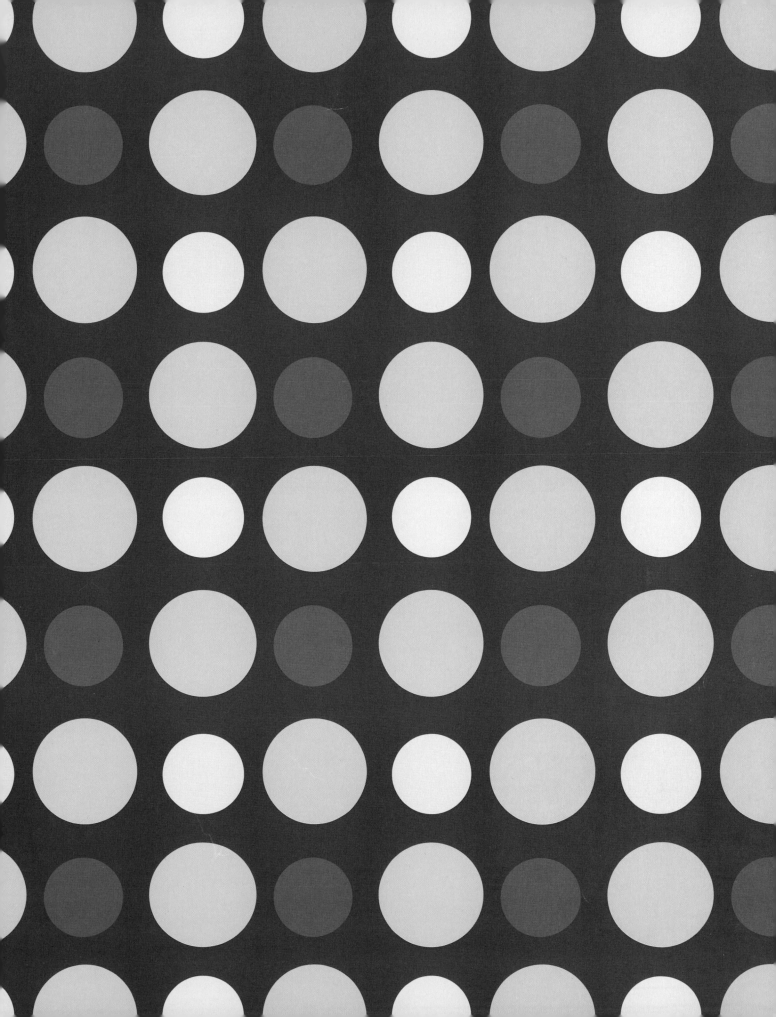

Disney Junior

Treasury

This edition published by Parragon Books Ltd in 2014

Parragon Books Ltd
Chartist House
15–17 Trim Street
Bath BA1 1HA, UK
www.parragon.com

ISBN 978-1-4723-5008-4

Printed in China

Disney Junior
Treasury

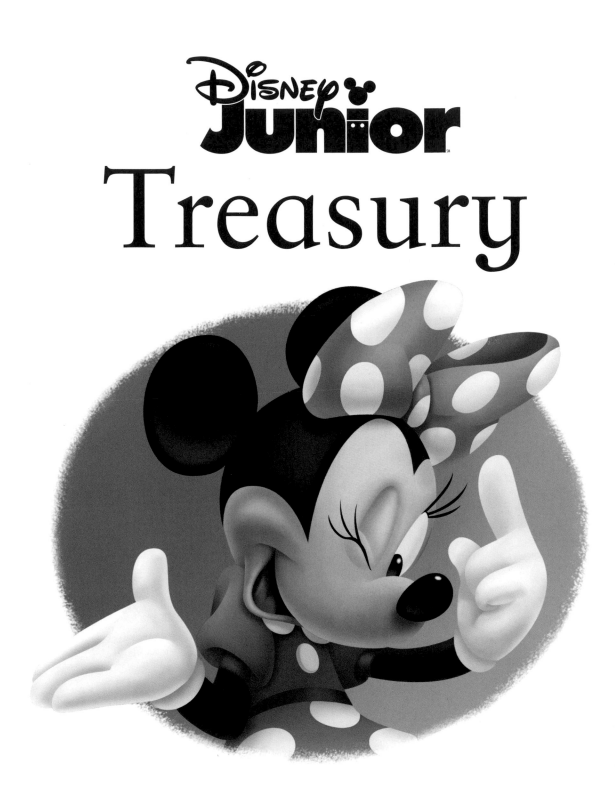

Bath • New York • Cologne • Melbourne • Delhi
Hong Kong • Shenzhen • Singapore • Amsterdam

This book belongs to

....

....

Contents

Super Adventure

Based on the episode written by Mark Seidenberg
Adapted by Bill Scollon
Illustrated by Loter, Inc.

"Hiya, everybody," says Mickey. "Welcome to the Clubhouse!"
Today, Mickey and his pals are pretending to be superheroes.

"Superheroes work together to save the day from supervillains,"
Mickey explains.

Donald pretends to be the bad guy.
"You'll never defeat me," he shouts.

The superheroes chase Donald every which way.

"Wait! We're supposed to work as a super-team," Mickey says.

But the heroes don't listen and end up in a jumble! Just then, a shadow falls over the gang.

"Gawrsh!" says Goofy. "It's a giant hot-dog balloon."

"That's an airship," says Mickey. "But what's it doing here?"

Suddenly, the airship zaps the Glove Balloon with a shrink ray!

Power-Pants Pete flies down. "Stay back," he warns. "I'm about to shrink everything in the Clubhouse World!"

Power-Pants Pete picks up the tiny Glove Balloon and flies off!
"We have to stop Pete from shrinking everything!" says Mickey.
Goofy scratches his head. "This is a super-problem," he says.
"Did someone say 'super'?" asks Professor Von Drake. "I have just
the thingamajig you need!"

VOOM!

The professor has a new invention.

"I call it the Super-Maker Machine," he says.

"It makes soup?" asks Goofy.

"No, Goofy," laughs the professor. "It will make real superheroes out of all of you."

"Super cheers," says Mickey. "That's just what we need!"

"Then step right in," the professor says.

"Now you all have super-fantastic powers!" the professor exclaims.
"But you'll have to work together to stop Power-Pants Pete."
"Don't worry," says Super Mickey. "The Clubhouse Heroes are ready!"

"One more thing," the professor adds. "You'll only have your powers for a little while. When your Superpower Bands turn red, your powers will go kaput."

"Then we'd better get going!" says Wonder Minnie.

Power-Pants Pete is about to shrink Minnie's Bow-tique!

Upsy Daisy has an idea. "I'll use my mind powers to push the airship."

Wonder Minnie has another idea. "My Super-Wonder Bows will stop Pete."

But nothing works.

"Your powers blocked each other," says Mickey.

Suddenly, Pete drops hundreds of rubber ducks!

Mickey calls for help. "Oh, Super Toodles."

Super Toodles has four Super Mouseketools – a giant hairdryer, a baseball glove, a big umbrella and a Mystery Mouseketool.

"Let's try the umbrella!" says Mickey.

The big umbrella does the trick. The rubber ducks bounce right off. But Pete shrinks Minnie's Bow-tique anyway and zooms off!

Pete's next target is the Eiffel Tower. The heroes have to hurry. Their Superpower Bands are turning red! Super Goofy and Dynamo Donald get all twisted and hit the airship. Pete falls to the ground!

"You're through, Power-Pants Pete!" says Super Mickey.

"I'm sorry," says Pete. "But the big boss made me do it!"

THUD!

The airship lands and out comes the big boss – Megamort!

"It's shrinking time," he says. Megamort makes Pete tiny with his shrink ray.

"Oh, that tickled," says Pete.

"Megamort!" says Minnie. "You're just a mean ol' meany villain."

Megamort nods. "I'm taking the Clubhouse World for myself!"

He jumps in the airship and takes off again.

"We have to catch Megamort," says Mickey. "Our powers are almost gone!"

Mickey and Super Power-Pup zoom into the sky and grab hold of the airship.

But Megamort traps them in a super-strong bubble!

"We need a Mouseketool," says Mickey. "Oh, Super Toodles!"

FOOSH!

Mickey chooses the giant hairdryer. It works! The hairdryer blows all the bubbles away. "Bye-bye, bubbles!" says Mickey.

Back on the ground, Tiny Pete is rolling down a hill!
The heroes try to catch him, but they trip over each other
and fall into a heap.

"Tiny Pete is rolling away and our Superpower Bands are
all red!" says Daisy.

In a flash, the Clubhouse Heroes
lose all their superpowers!

Up in the airship, Megamort takes aim at the Clubhouse.
Mickey tries to stop him, but he loses his powers, too.

ZAP!

As Mickey falls towards the ground, Megamort zaps
him and the Clubhouse!

Tiny Mickey tells Pluto to go and find the Clubhouse Heroes.

Megamort scoops up Mickey and the Clubhouse
and takes them up to the airship.

Minnie and the rest of the heroes are still trying to save Tiny Pete. But Pete hits a bump and is launched into the air!

"We have to catch him," shouts Minnie. "Oh, Super Toodles!"

Minnie chooses the baseball glove. She runs to catch Pete, but she's too far away. Minnie tosses the glove to Daisy, but she's not close enough, either. Goofy grabs the glove and makes the catch!

"We did it," says Minnie. "We worked together as a team!"

All at once, the gang is turned back into superheroes!
"When we work together," says Minnie, "we're super-duper!"
Minnie looks up. "Uh-oh. Megamort has captured Mickey!"
"We gotta save him," says Goofy. "Oh, Super Toodles!"

The gang picks the Mystery Mouseketool. It's a super-jet!

"Up and away," says Minnie. "Let's save the day!"

The heroes plan to work together to rescue Mickey.

Goofy and Donald sneak aboard the airship and find the shrunken Clubhouse World. They quickly gather up all the bubbles. Megamort tries to stop them, but Tiny Mickey trips him up just in time!

FWING!

The heroes bring the airship to a sudden stop. Goofy, Donald and Mickey tumble out and land right in the super-jet! But the airship springs a leak and flies out of control.

"Megamort needs help!" shouts Mickey.

"But he's a villain," says Goofy.

"He still needs saving," says Mickey. "And that's what heroes do!"

Pluto helps Wonder Minnie tie up the airship with her Super-Wonder Bows. Then Donald and Goofy grab the ribbons and pull. Soon the rest of the gang joins them. Everyone works together to pull the airship to the ground.

"We did it!" they shout.

Megamort scrambles out of the flattened airship.

"After all I did, I can't believe you rescued me," he says. "Thank you."

"You're welcome, Mr Megamort," says Goofy.

"I'm really Mortimer Mouse," Megamort reveals. "I'm your new neighbour."

ZAP!

"Well, you weren't acting very neighbourly," Minnie points out.

Mortimer agrees. He reverses the shrink ray and returns Mickey and Pete to their normal sizes!

Then Mortimer un-shrinks the whole Clubhouse World.

"I'm sorry," he says. "I thought if I took what you had, I'd be happy."

"The Clubhouse is all about having friends," says Mickey.

"That's just it," Mortimer admits. "I don't have any friends."

"You do now!" says Goofy.

"That's super!" Mortimer says.

"It's more than super," says Mickey. "It's super-duper!"

The Mermaid Dives In

By Sheila Sweeny Higginson
Based on the episode by Kent Redeker
Based on the series created by Chris Nee
Illustrated by Character Building Studio
and the Disney Storybook Artists

Finally, summer is here! Doc McStuffins can't wait to play in the park with her friends.

Mum smooths suncream on Doc's skin. Now she's ready for some fun in the sun!

"Is it okay if I take my toys and play in the wading pool?" Doc asks.

"Sure," says Mum. "I'll keep an eye on you."

Doc wheels her wagon to the wading pool. Her stethoscope begins to glow!

"Hi, guys!" Doc says as her friends come to life.

"I finally get to go swimming!" Stuffy cheers. He jumps into the pool. Doc catches Stuffy in the nick of time.

"You and Lambie can't go in the water," Doc laughs. "You're not water toys."

But there *is* a water toy at the other side of the pool. She has long, flowing hair and a shimmering tail.

"It's a mermaid!" Lambie gasps. "They're like the princesses of the sea!"

Doc and Stuffy walk over to the other side of the pool. Then Doc brings the mermaid to life with her magic stethoscope.

"Hello," the mermaid says. "My name is Melinda."

"I'd love to watch you swim," Lambie says shyly.

"Very well," Melinda says. "Prepare to be amazed!"

Doc takes a hoop out of the wagon and hands it to Surfer Girl.

"Take this to the centre of the pool so Melinda can jump through it,"
Doc says.

"Here I go!" Melinda calls. "It will be the most amazing water leap you've ever seen!"

Melinda splashes into the pool. But then she disappears!

"Hey, like, where'd she go?" asks Surfer Girl.

"I see her!" Bronty calls. "She's at the bottom of the pool!"

Doc reaches into the pool and rescues Melinda.

"Did you mean to do that?" Doc asks her.

"No," Melinda says. "I don't know why I sank to the bottom."

"I don't know, either," says Doc. "I'm worried something might be wrong with you."

"Wrong? I don't think so," says Melinda. "Mermaids are perfect."

"No one is perfect," Doc explains. "I think I should give you a check-up."

First, Doc checks Melinda's heart with her stethoscope.
"Your heartbeat sounds just as pretty as you are," says Doc.
Then she listens to Melinda's lungs.
"Your lungs sound good, too," Doc adds.

"Now I'm going to check your tail," Doc says. She asks Melinda to push with her tail.

Melinda tries, but she can't do it. "Is something wrong with me?" she asks.

Doc shrugs. "Has anyone ever wound up your winder-upper?"

"I didn't even know I had one!" Melinda says.

A-ha! Doc McStuffins has a diagnosis.

"You have a case of Stuck-Winder-Upperitis," she tells Melinda.

"Is that serious?" Melinda asks.

Doc shakes her head. "I can fix it right up!" She works on Melinda's winder-upper until it's unstuck. "Got it!" Doc says.

Then Lambie winds the winder and Melinda's tail starts to flap!

"My tail is flapping!" Melinda cheers. "Get ready for a wonderful mermaid leaping show!"

Melinda splashes into the pool, but she sinks again!
"Oh, dear!" she cries. "I'm going down!"

Doc reaches into the pool and rescues Melinda again.

"Oh, Doc!" Melinda cries. "I'm a mermaid! I should be able to swim and leap and do all sorts of tricks. But I just keep sinking."

"Did you have this problem when you took swimming lessons?" Doc asks.

"What's that?" Melinda wonders.

"That's when someone teaches you how to swim. You took them, right?"

"No," Melinda says. "Do I need swimming lessons?"

"Everyone should take swimming lessons," Doc explains.
"I had so much fun learning to swim!"
Melinda is excited and wants to take swimming lessons, too!

"Let me handle this one," says Surfer Girl. "I used to be a lifeguard, so I gave swimming lessons all the time!"

First, Surfer Girl shows Melinda how to stroke with her arms.

"That's it!" says Surfer Girl.

Then she shows Melinda how to kick with her tail.

"Great job," Surfer Girl says.

Soon Melinda starts to swim on her own.

"You're an amazing swimmer!" Lambie calls.

"I'm so glad I took swimming lessons," Melinda says.

"I finally feel like a real mermaid!"

This time, when Melinda the Mermaid leaps through the hoop, she swims like a real mermaid, too!

Ahoy, Izzy!

Written by Marcy Kelman
Based on the episode written by Nicole Dubuc
Illustrated by Character Building Studio
and the Disney Storybook Artists

Ahoy, mateys! Do you want to join my pirate crew? Then just say the pirate password, "Yo-ho-ho!" As part of my crew, you'll need to learn the Never Land pirate pledge.

Today's Pirate Pledge

A good pirate never takes another person's property!

"Want to play Ahoy 'n' Seek, mateys?" Jake asks.

Cubby scratches his head. "Ahoy 'n' Seek? What's that?"

"A game where someone hides while the others count to ten," says Izzy. "And when you find the person hiding, you shout 'AHOY!'"

"That sounds like fun!" says Cubby.

"And the best part? When you're done counting, you blow this horn, which sounds just like the Never Sea whale," explains Jake.

BOW-OOOH-GAH!

"What was that noise?" says Captain Hook, aiming his spyglass at Never Land. "Why, it's an earsplitting, noise-making thingamajig!"

"Well, blow me down! That's a sure way to get everyone's attention," laughs Smee.

"I must have it, Smee!" snarls Hook. "Hurry, let's go ashore!"

"Ready, guys? I'm going to find the best hiding place ever," calls Izzy.

"Okay, we'll start counting," says Cubby.

1, 2, 3, 4, 5,

"We're done counting, Cubby!" Jake says.
"Blow the Ahoy 'n' Seek horn!"

BOW-OOOH-GAH!

Jake, Skully and Cubby set out
in search of Izzy's hiding place.

"Barnacles!" exclaims Cubby.
"Where could she have gone?"

"Yo-ho, I spy a clue!" cries Jake. "See how there's a path of flattened grass here? She must have pushed the grass down when she walked on it."

"Over there, behind that tree!" shouts Cubby.

"AHOY, IZZY!"

Jake giggles. "That's not Izzy. It's a flamingo!"
"Aw, coconuts!" says Cubby. "Now where should
we look?"

"Say, me hearties," squawks Skully. "We haven't checked Bucky."

"Great idea, Skully!" says Jake.

The friends head towards their trusty ship.

With Jake and his crew busy looking for Izzy, Hook and Smee come ashore so Hook can nab the horn.

"Oh my, Cap'n," says Smee. "Aren't those sea pups using the noise-making thingamajig for their hiding game?"

Hook smiles slyly. "Do you see a puny pipsqueak anywhere in sight? Finders keepers!"

Meanwhile, on board Bucky, Jake thinks they've found Izzy. "Look, sticking out of the cupboard – it's Izzy's bandana!"

They rush to the cupboard door.

"AHOY, IZZY!"

"Crackers!" squawks Skully.

"It's just a mop."

Just then, the sound of the Ahoy 'n' Seek horn bellows across the island.

BOW-OOOH-GAH!

"Who could be blowing the horn?" asks Cubby.

Izzy darts out of her hiding spot. "I bet it's that sneaky snook Captain Hook!"

"Yo-ho, let's go and get our horn!" shouts Jake.

"Barnacles and bilge water! You blew it!" shouts Hook.
"Why, yes, Cap'n, I did!" says Smee proudly. "I just put
my mouth on the opening here, and...."

"No, no, no, you blithering buffoon – I mean you blew
our cover. Now those meddling swabs will know that we've
stolen their treasure."

Smee realizes his mistake. "Oh, dear!"

When Hook sees Jake and his crew coming towards him, he grabs the horn from Smee and starts to run. "Well, blow me down!" Hook shouts frantically.

The playful Never Sea whale is more than happy to grant
Captain Hook's wish. He sprays a powerful blast of water
right at the captain and blows him down!

"Yay-hey, no way!" Izzy springs into action when she sees the Ahoy 'n' Seek horn fly up into the air. "This looks like an emergency. I'd better use my Pixie Dust."

When Jake and Cubby see Izzy catch the horn in mid-air, they cheer,

"AHOY, IZZY!"

"Well, that sure was a blast!" jokes Cubby.

"Stealing is never a good idea, Hook!" says Izzy.

"I guess your plan was all washed up from the start, Cap'n," says Smee.

"For solving pirate problems today, we earned eleven Gold Doubloons!" Jake says.

"Playing Ahoy 'n' Seek was awesome!" Cubby says.

"Aye, and from the looks of it, the cap'n is still having a whale of a time!" squawks Skully.

BOW-OOOH-GAH!

Save Me, Smee!

Written by Melinda LaRose

Illustrated by Character Building Studio
and the Disney Storybook Art Team

Ahoy, mateys! Do you want to join my pirate crew? Then just say the pirate password, "Yo-ho-ho!" As part of my crew, you'll need to learn the Never Land pirate pledge.

Today's Pirate Pledge

A pirate is always willing to help out a friend.

"Blast it, Smee! I didn't sleep a wink all night," says Hook.
"Captain Cuddly is missing! You know I can't go beddy-bye
without my teddy bear."

Just then, Hook spots a teeny, tiny treasure chest.

"Why, it's me first treasure chest from when I was just
a wee little pirate."

There's a treasure map inside the chest!

"We have to go across Slippery Snake River and through Crumble Canyon. Then X marks the spot at – gulp! – Skull Rock," says Smee. "Those are the most perilous places in all of Never Land."

"So what?" says Hook. "There's treasure and I want it."

"Be careful, Mr Smee," says Jake. "You're heading for Slippery Snake River!"

Smee nods. "I'm afraid the captain's after treasure."

"We could follow in case there's any trouble," says Izzy.

"Oh, you sea pups are so kind," says Smee.

"Danger, schmanger," says Hook. "It's just a river." Hook jumps on the back of a slippery snake.

BOING, BOING, SPLASH!

"Save me, Smee!" calls the captain. "Oh dear, oh dear! Right away, Cap'n!"

BOING, BOING, SPLASH!

Smee falls into the river, too!

"We have to help Hook and Smee," says Jake.

"But how can we get to them?" asks Cubby. "The snakes are too slippery to jump across!"

"We'd better think of something quick," says Jake.

Izzy makes a lasso and tosses it to Smee. "Mr Smee, catch!" she calls.

Then Jake and the crew pull Smee and Hook to shore. "Great work, Iz," says Jake.

"Thank you, sea pups," whispers Smee.

"See? That wasn't dangerous at all," says Hook as he staggers to the shore and falls down.

"Oh, my," says Smee. "What do you say we go back to the Jolly Roger now, Cap'n? I'll make you a nice cup of tea."

"Never!" says Hook. "Crumble Canyon awaits!"

"Crackers! Hook and Smee are going across that narrow pass," says Skully.

"Be ready to lend a hand, crew," says Jake.

"See, Smee? This is a breeze," says Captain Hook.

"I don't even know why they call it Crumble Canyon."

"Well, sir," says Smee, "it's because the sides of the canyon tend to ..."

"Aiieeee!" yells Hook as the ground beneath him collapses.

"... crumble," finishes Smee.

"Save me, Smee!" yells Hook.

"I gotcha, Cap'n," says Smee.

"But who has *you?*" asks Hook.

"Ahh!" Smee starts to fall over the edge of the canyon.

Skully swoops in and grabs Smee.

"I got you, Skully," calls Cubby.

"And I've got *you*," says Izzy.

"Come on, crew! Heave ho! Heave ho!" calls Jake.

Together, they hoist Hook and Smee to safety.

"Are you ... okay ... sir?" Smee pants.

"I'll be better when I have that treasure," says Hook.

"Are you sure you don't want to go home? I'll make hot chocolate with those little marshmallows you like so much."

"I do love little marshmallows," says Hook, "but Skull Rock and treasure await!"

"Hook can't go to Skull Rock," says Cubby. "It's way too dangerous."

"He'll never give up looking for that treasure," says Smee.

"Unless," says Izzy, "there was an even *better* treasure for him to find."

"Great idea, Iz," says Jake. "We can make a new treasure for Hook to find. Somewhere nice and safe."

"But we don't have any treasure," says Cubby.

"I know where there's a treasure that the cap'n will just love," says Smee.

"Skully, send word to Sharky and Bones to prepare the treasure," says Jake.

"Aye-aye!" Skully says.

"Cubby, can you make a new map?" Jake asks.

"Aye-aye, Jake!" says Cubby.

"Now to get Hook to take the bait," says Jake.
"Hey, Izzy," he says loudly enough for Hook to hear.
"I can't believe we found a map to the most awesome
  treasure in all of Never Land!"
  "Yeah. Lucky Captain Hook isn't around to take our
map to the really awesome treasure," says Izzy.

"Ha! You can't fool the great Captain Hook. I'll be taking the map *and* the treasure," says Hook.

"Aw, coconuts," says Cubby, winking at Smee. "You tricked us again."

"We'll never find the awesome treasure now," says Skully.

"I don't believe me eyes," says Hook. "The treasure is aboard the Jolly Roger!"

"Oh, is that so?" asks Smee innocently.

"The most awesome treasure in all of Never Land – right on me own ship," says Hook happily.

"Look alive," says Hook. "There be treasure aboard."

"X marks the spot," says Smee.

It's Captain Cuddly!

"Oh, my little cuddly wuddly! You are the greatest treasure in all of Never Land. Yes, you are," says Hook.

"He had a little rip," says Bones, "but I fixed him right up."
"Did you have an ouchy, Captain Cuddly?" asks Hook.
"Whew!" says Smee. "Now that we're home, I imagine you won't be needing any more rescuing today, Cap'n."

"Rescuing? What do you mean rescuing?" says Hook.
"The great Captain Hook has never needed to be rescued.
Isn't that right, Captain Cuddly?"

Splash! Hook accidentally knocks his bear overboard.

"Bear overboard!" yells Hook. He dives into the water ...
and finds his bear in the arms of the Tick Tock Croc!
"Save me, Smee! And Captain Cuddly, too!"
"Right away, Cap'n," Smee says as he jumps into the water.

Blooming Bows

Based on the television episode written by Robert Ramirez
Adapted by Nancy Parent
Illustrated by Loter, Inc.

It's a busy day at Minnie's Bow-tique. Minnie and Daisy are getting ready for two special visitors.

"Daisy," says Minnie, "did you find the camera?"

"Not yet," replies Daisy. "But I know I have it
here somewhere!"

Daisy turns around. "Here it is, Daisy," says Minnie. "Thanks!" says Daisy. "Now I'll be able to get a good picture of you and the twins."

Just then, Minnie hears giggling. "Get ready!" she cries.
"Here they come!"

"Ta-daaah!" Millie and Melody shout.

"I'm Purple Posy!" says Melody.
"And I'm Rosie Posy!" says Millie.

Minnie greets her twin nieces while Daisy snaps
a picture of them.

"Hold that pose, pretty posies!" cries Daisy.
The twins twirl and spin and pose for the camera.
"Oh!" says Minnie. "You both look simply adorable!"

As the girls twirl around to show off their costumes, some of the flower petals fall off.

Daisy snaps away as Cuckoo-Loca flies in for a closer look.

"So, are you all set for the Posy Pageant?" asks Cuckoo-Loca, watching the twins from Daisy's shoulder.

"We sure are, Cuckoo-Loca!" says Millie. "Come on, Melody, let's show them our posy prance dance!"

As the girls dance, more and more paper petals fall to the floor.

"Is that supposed to happen?" whispers Cuckoo-Loca, pointing to all the petals on the floor.

The girls sing:

"We can dance! We can sing!
On the first day of spring!
But you better make room,
'Cause it's time to bloom!"

"Oh, my," Minnie says.

"That bloom went *ka-boom!*" adds Cuckoo-Loca.

The twins stare sadly at all the petals on the floor.

"Uh-oh," says Melody. "I guess the glue wasn't dry."

"I'll say," says Cuckoo-Loca.

"Don't worry, girls," Minnie says. "We'll fix these right up."

"Oh, please hurry, Aunt Minnie!" says Melody.

"Or else we can't be in the pageant!" cries Millie.

"I've got the sticky-wicky goo-glue!" Daisy cries.
"Good thinking, Daisy!" says Minnie.

Minnie watches as Daisy glues the petals back on. "Let's see, this pink one goes here, this purple one goes there ... wait ... is that right?" asks Daisy.

"Daisy!" says Melody. "I'm Purple Posy!
She's Rosie Posy!"

Millie and Melody look down sadly at their messy, mixed-up costumes.

Minnie gives the twins a big hug. "There, there, now, girls," she says. "I'll figure something out."

"But how?" asks Melody. "It's a flower show, Aunt Minnie, not a bow show!"

Minnie thinks and thinks. She really wants to help her nieces!

Suddenly, Minnie has an idea. "Girls!" she calls. "Follow me!"
Grabbing an armful of fabric, Minnie leads the girls to the
dressing room.

While Minnie cuts fabric and ties ribbons, the twins giggle excitedly. Daisy and Cuckoo-Loca can't wait to see what Minnie is creating.

Soon, Minnie reappears.
"Ladies and gentle-bird, introducing our
favourite flowers: Rosie Posy and Purple Posy!"

"Pop-up posies!" cries Daisy. "And no glue needed!"
"Now that's what I call getting out of a sticky
situation," says Cuckoo-Loca.

Millie and Melody are so happy! They can't stop smiling!
Minnie gathers the twins. "Come on, my little posies.
It's showtime!"

"Hey, girls!" Daisy calls, holding up her camera.
"Say *posies*!"

The twins stand with Minnie and all three smile
for Daisy's photo.

Millie and Melody wave goodbye as they run
out the door.

"Wow, Minnie!" says Daisy, smiling at her friend.
"Who knew you had such flower power?"

"It's like I always say, Daisy," says Minnie.
"There's no business like *bow* business!"

The Royal Slumber Party

Written by Catherine Hapka

Based on the episode by Erica Rothschild

Illustrated by Character Building Studio

and the Disney Storybook Artists

Sofia and Amber are having a royal sleepover tonight!

"This is where we'll be sleeping," Amber says.

"The observatory? We get to sleep under the stars!" Sofia cries.

"It's a royal slumber party," Amber says. "Everything has to be amazing."

Sofia's two best friends, Ruby and Jade, are coming!
Amber is shocked. "You invited some village girls?
You're a princess now. You should only invite princesses
to royal parties!"

"But Ruby and Jade are fun!" Sofia assures Amber. "You'll see."

The royal herald's trumpet sounds. "They're here!" Sofia cries. Amber's friends, Princess Hildegard and Princess Clio, step out of their coaches. Behind them are Jade and Ruby in an oxcart. "I can't believe we're here!" Jade exclaims, hugging Sofia. "We're so excited!" Ruby adds.

It's time for the party to start! The princesses change into fancy nightgowns. Ruby and Jade giggle as they roll their hair in pine cone curlers – just like at home.

"We're at a royal sleepover!" they chant, pulling Sofia up to join their silly dance.

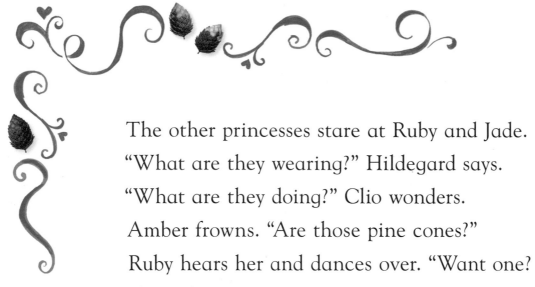

The other princesses stare at Ruby and Jade.

"What are they wearing?" Hildegard says.

"What are they doing?" Clio wonders.

Amber frowns. "Are those pine cones?"

Ruby hears her and dances over. "Want one? We brought extras."

Amber marches over to Sofia. "Sofia! Pine cones are not part of a perfect princess slumber party."

Sofia's worried. She wants her new sister and her old friends to like each other.

"They can fit in," she says. "They just need a little help."

Sofia has a great idea. "How would you two like a royal makeover?" she asks her friends.

Ruby and Jade squeal with excitement!

Baileywick and Sofia's woodland friends help out. They fix the girls' hair and dress them in pretty gowns and tiaras.

Sofia makes her friends cover their eyes. Then she leads them to a mirror. "Open your eyes," she says.

Jade and Ruby gasp when they see themselves.

"I'm a princess!" Ruby exclaims.

"Me, too!" calls Jade.

Next it's time for party activities. First comes fan decorating.
Ruby and Jade have fun, but their fans don't look very princessy.
Then the girls play a game of Pin the Tail on the Unicorn.
"Ooh! Ooh!" Jade says. "Can I go first?"
But Jade ends up nowhere near the unicorn!

After that, the girls watch Cedric, the royal sorcerer, put on a magic puppet show in the banquet hall. During the show, James, Sofia's brother, walks in with a message for the girls.

"Prince James!" Jade and Ruby squeal, rushing towards him. They're thrilled to see the friendly prince!

Jade and Ruby are so excited, they accidentally knock over the chocolate milk fountain. Oops! Chocolate milk splashes onto Amber's nightgown. She is furious!

"We're so, so, so sorry!" Ruby says to Amber.

"So sorry," Jade adds.

Amber walks off in a huff while Sofia shakes her head sadly.

Baileywick hurries Jade and Ruby away to get cleaned up.
Then James tells the girls it's time for dancing in the throne room.

"Let's go," Amber says. "Maybe we can enjoy five minutes of our party without Sofia's friends making a mess."

Now Sofia's even more
worried! She goes off to
find her friends.

"I want you both to fit
in with the princesses,"
Sofia explains.

"We look just like them
now, don't we?" Jade says.

"Yes," Sofia says.
"But princesses don't talk
so much, or laugh so loudly,
or make so many messes."

Jade frowns. "We were just having fun."

"We're sorry," Ruby adds quickly. "We'll try to act more like Amber and the other princesses."

"Thank you!" Sofia is relieved. Now she's sure everyone will get along!

Sofia and her friends join the others in the throne room.
But Ruby and Jade don't know how to waltz. All they can do
is stand there and watch the princesses dance.

After a while, they tell Sofia that they want to go home.

"But you're finally fitting in!" Sofia cries. "And you're not embarrassing me anymore!"

"I'm sorry if we talk too much and laugh too loudly for your fancy new friends," says Jade. "Maybe we shouldn't be friends anymore!"

Ruby takes Jade's arm and together they rush out
of the room.

"Don't worry about them," Hildegard tells Sofia.
"You're with us now."

Sofia goes after her friends but finds her mother instead. "I was trying to help Jade and Ruby fit in," she explains. "But I just made them feel bad."

"A true princess treats people with kindness, Sofia," Queen Miranda says gently. "If someone is your friend, you should like them for who they are."

Sofia knows her mother is right. She runs outside and finds her friends just as they are about to leave.

"I'm sorry about the way I acted," she says. "Please let me make it up to you. We can have our own slumber party – just the three of us!"

Jade and Ruby think for a moment and finally agree to stay.

Soon Sofia and her friends are in her room, having a great
time. They laugh – loudly. They talk – a lot. They roll pine cones
in their hair and perch tiaras on top.

Meanwhile, Amber and her friends go back to the observatory.

"Finally, it's just us princesses," Amber says.

"This is a perfect party," Hildegard agrees with a yawn.

There's a long silence. The princesses are really bored.

"You know," Clio speaks up, "Sofia's friends were kind of fun."

A moment later, Amber and her friends knock on Sofia's door.

"Um, do you have room for a few more princesses?" asks Amber.

Sofia looks at Jade and Ruby. "What do you think?"

"The more, the merrier," Ruby says with a smile.

Sofia and Amber end up having the perfect sleepover with friends – old and new!

The End

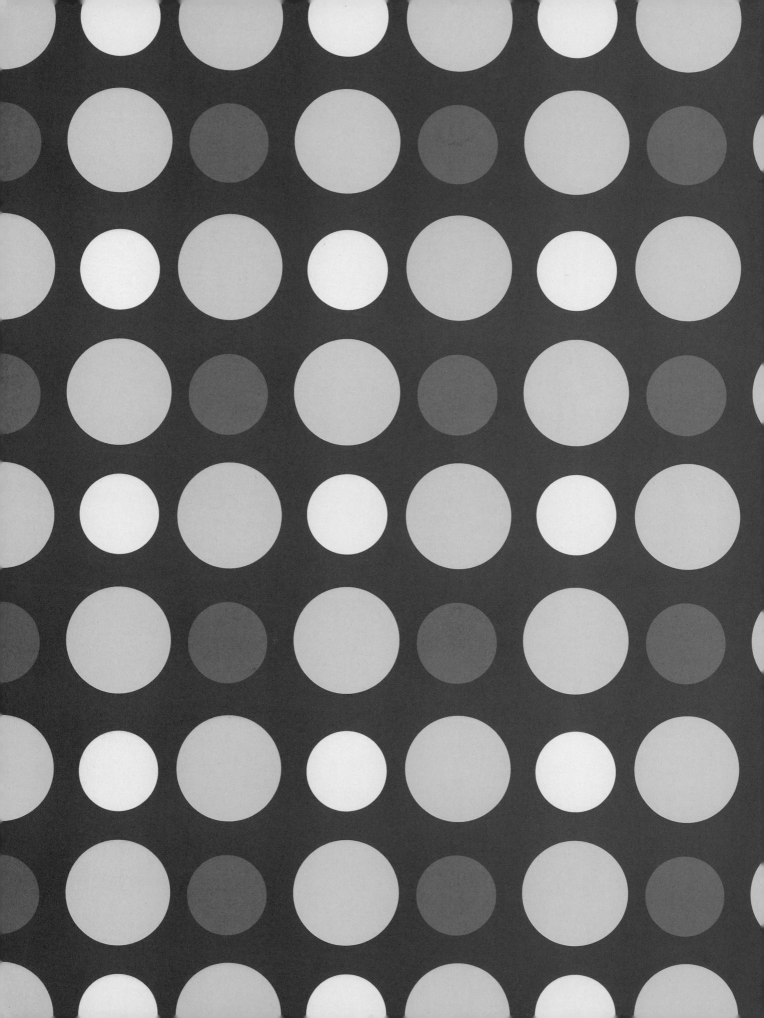

Goodbye!